W9-CIG-114

A NOTE TO PARENTS

Congratulations on choosing the best in educational materials for your child. By selecting top-quality McGraw-Hill products, you can be assured that the concepts used in our books will reinforce and enhance the skills that are being taught in classrooms nationwide.

And what better way to get young readers excited than with Mercer Mayer's Little Critter, a character loved by children everywhere? Our First Readers offer simple and engaging stories about Little Critter that children can read on their own. Each level incorporates reading skills, colorful illustrations, and challenging activities.

Level 1 – The stories are simple and use repetitive language. Illustrations are highly supportive.
Level 2 - The stories begin to grow in complexity. Language is still repetitive, but it is mixed with more challenging vocabulary.
Level 3 - The stories are more complex. Sentences are longer and more varied.

To help your child make the most of this book, look at the first few pictures in the story and discuss what is happening. Ask your child to predict where the story is going. Then, once your child has read the story, have him or her review the word list and do the activities. This will reinforce vocabulary words from the story and build reading comprehension.

You are your child's first and most influential teacher. No one knows your child the way you do. Tailor your time together to reinforce a newly acquired skill or to overcome a temporary stumbling block. Praise your child's progress and ideas, take delight in his or her imagination, and most of all, enjoy your time together!

Library of Congress Cataloging-in-Publication Data

Mayer, Mercer, 1943-
Our tree house / by Mercer Mayer.
          p. cm. -- (First readers, skills and practice)
"Level 3, Grades 1-2."
Summary: When Little Critter's friends are too busy to join him in his new tree house, he finally asks Little Sister to play with him.
ISBN 1-57768-636-5 (HC), 1-57768-833-3 (PB)
[1. Tree house—Fiction. 2. Brothers and sisters—Fiction.] I. Title. II. Series.
PZ7.M462 Ow 2003
[E]--dc21
        2002008748

Mc Graw Hill **Children's Publishing**

Text Copyright © 2003 McGraw-Hill Children's Publishing.
Art Copyright © 2003 Mercer Mayer.

Send all inquiries to:
McGraw-Hill Children's Publishing
8787 Orion Place
Columbus, OH 43240-4027

Printed in the United States of America.

1-57768-636-5

 A Big Tuna Trading Company, LLC/J. R. Sansevere Book

1 2 3 4 5 6 7 8 9 10 PHXBK 08 07 06 05 04 03

FIRST READERS

Level **3**   Grades **1–2**

OUR TREE HOUSE

by Mercer Mayer

 McGraw Hill **Children's Publishing**

Columbus, Ohio

Today, Dad and I built a tree house.
I couldn't wait to invite
my friends over to see it.

4

Little Sister wanted to come up, too.
"Tree houses are for big kids," I told her.

First, I went to Gabby's house.
"Do you want to come up
  to my tree house?" I asked.
"I can't," she said.
"I'm helping my dad bake cookies."

Then, I went to Maurice
and Molly's house.
"Do you want to come up
to my tree house?" I asked.
"We can't," they said.
"We're going to the zoo with our mom."

After that, I headed over
to Malcolm's house.
"Do you want to come up
to my tree house?" I asked.
"I can't," he said. "I'm helping
my grandma with our yard sale."

3 FOR
1.00

5¢

SING

ALBUMS CHEAP!

$1.00

25¢

11

Finally, I went to Gator's house.
"Do you want to come up
to my tree house?" I asked.
Gator sneezed.
"I can't," said Gator. "I'm sick."

13

When I got home, I asked Little Sister if
she wanted to come up to the tree house.
She told me she was busy.

"We can play any game
you want," I said.
"Okay," said Little Sister.
"I'll be back."

Little Sister came back with a big box.
She pulled out her dolls and her tea set.
"You can pour the tea, Little Critter,"
she said.

So, we had a tea party with cookies
and chips for everyone.
"I guess tree houses aren't just
for big kids," I said.
"Tree houses are for fun!"

Word List

Read each word in the lists below. Then, find it in the story. Now, make up a new sentence using the word. Say your sentence out loud.

<table>
<tr><td>Words I Know</td><td>Challenge Words</td></tr>
<tr><td>house</td><td>built</td></tr>
<tr><td>friends</td><td>couldn't</td></tr>
<tr><td>cookies</td><td>sneezed</td></tr>
<tr><td>everyone</td><td>busy</td></tr>
<tr><td></td><td>pour</td></tr>
<tr><td></td><td>guess</td></tr>
</table>

Capitalization: People's Names

A person's or a critter's name always begins with a capital letter.

Example: Gator is Little Critter's friend.

Look at Little Critter's friends below. Point to the correct name for each picture.

maurice

Tiger

Gabby

molly

Maurice

tiger

gabby

Molly

Contractions

We can put two words together to make one shorter word. The shorter word is called a contraction. An apostrophe is used in place of the letters that are taken out.

This is an apostrophe: ⌐'⌐

Examples: were not ⟶ weren't

we will ⟶ we'll

they are ⟶ they're

are not ⟶ aren't

Count all the contractions in the story. Careful, some names have apostrophes but are not contractions. How many did you find?

20

Look at the words in the first column. Then point to the correct contraction in the same row.

can not →cann't   cant'   can't

it is ⟶ it's   it is   its'

did not → didn't   din't   didnt'

I am ⟶ I'am   I'm   Im'

I will ⟶ Iw'll   I'll   Ill

you are →you're   y'ar   youer

Our House

The sound you hear in the middle of our and house is spelled by the letters ou.

Read the words below and say them out loud. Then, point to the words with the same ou sound as our and house.

ground	would
bought	outside
count	found
tour	cloud
pound	pour
around	should

Comprehension Check

The sentences below are from the story, but they are in the wrong order. Point to each statement in the order that it occurs in the story.

1. Little Critter goes to Gator's house, but Gator is sick.

2. Little Critter goes to Malcolm's house, but Malcolm is helping his grandma with the yard sale.

3. Little Critter and Dad build a tree house.

4. Little Critter goes to Gabby's house, but she is helping her dad make cookies.

5. Little Critter and Little Sister have a tea party in the tree house.

Hint: Statement number 3 happened first.

Answer Key

page 19
Capitalization: People's Names

 Tiger

 Gabby

 Maurice

 Molly

page 20
Contractions

Did you count 11? If so, then you are correct! Good job!

page 21
Contractions

can't

it's

didn't

I'm

I'll

you're

page 22
Our House

ground

count

pound

around

outside

found

cloud

page 23
Comprehension Check

3. Little Critter and Dad build a tree house.

4. Little Critter goes to Gabby's house, but she is helping her dad make cookies.

2. Little Critter goes to Malcolm's house, but Malcolm is helping his grandma with the yard sale.

1. Little Critter goes to Gator's house, but Gator is sick.

5. Little Critter and Little Sister have a tea party in the tree house.